Dog Watch

BOOK TWO

Dog-Napped!

Dog Watch

Keeping the town of Pembrook
safe for people and dogs!

BOOK ONE:
Trouble in Pembrook

BOOK TWO:
Dog-Napped!

Coming Soon:
BOOK THREE:
Danger at Snow Hill

Dog Watch

BOOK TWO

Dog-Napped!

By Mary Casanova
Illustrated by Omar Rayyan

Aladdin Paperbacks
New York London Toronto Sydney

ALADDIN PAPERBACKS
An imprint of Simon & Schuster
Children's Publishing Division
1230 Avenue of the Americas, New York, NY 10020
Text copyright © 2006 by Mary Casanova
Illustrations copyright © 2006 by Omar Rayyan
All rights reserved, including the right of reproduction
in whole or in part in any form.
ALADDIN PAPERBACKS and colophon are trademarks
of Simon & Schuster, Inc.
Designed by Tom Daly
The text of this book was set in Gazette.
Manufactured in the United States of America
First Aladdin Paperbacks edition August 2006
2 4 6 8 10 9 7 5 3 1
Library of Congress Control Number 2005930110
ISBN-13: 978-0-689-86811-5
ISBN-10: 0-689-86811-1

Dedicated

to the dogs of Ranier, Minnesota—
past, present, and future

And

to Kate, Eric, and Charlie—
and to our family dogs, who have
brought us tears and trouble,
laughter and love
over the years

True:

On the edge of a vast northern Minnesota lake sits a quiet little village where dogs are allowed to roam free. Free, that is, until they get in trouble. One report of a tipped garbage can, nonstop barking, or car chasing, and the village clerk thumbs through doggie mugshots, identifies the dog from its photo, and places a round sticker on the culprit's page. Then she phones the dog's owner. Too many stickers and the troublesome dog is ordered to stay home—tethered to a chain or locked inside its house or yard. No more roaming, and no more adventures with the other dogs of the village.

A Bad Omen

One fall afternoon, when crisp air buffed hanging apples to a rosy red, and pumpkins appeared on doorsteps around the village, Kito and Chester napped outside. On a fuzzy plaid blanket, they slept soundly on either side of Mr. Hollinghorst.

Thud!

Startled awake, Kito sprang to his feet, his back hairs raised. He braced himself for trouble.

"It's okay, fella," said Mr. H, setting down his pen and scanning the deck of their cedar-shingled house. "A bird just hit our window. Poor thing. Every fall, that mountain ash tree fills with berries and attracts hungry cedar waxwings. They eat so much they get dizzy," he said, "and fly into windows."

Kito relaxed, shook his coat, and stretched.

Lying on his back, Chester woke up. Or his nose woke him. His round black nose twitched. He *snuffle, snuffle, snuffed.* Finally, his eyes shot open. "What is it? I smell something!"

"You always smell something," Kito said. "A bird hit the window, that's all." He started toward the lifeless little waxwing beside the house, but before he reached it, a raven swooped across his path and landed close to the dead bird. The scraggly black raven cocked its head, ruffled its wings, then snatched the little waxwing in its beak and flew off with it across the bay.

"Well, I'll be darned," Kito said.

Mr. H seemed to understand his words, though Kito knew his owner couldn't really

hear dog-talk. "Huh. Never saw anything like that … a raven preying on another bird," said Mr H. "Almost seems like a bad omen."

"Omen?" Chester asked Kito. "What does he mean, an omen? Is that like what they say after a prayer at dinner?"

"It means a portent of things to come."

"Portent? You mean, 'important'?"

Kito shook his head. "No, a sign." It was tough being the only dog in Pembrook who could read. He was always having to explain everything without giving away his source of information. "A sign of things to come."

"Good things or bad?" Chester asked, wrinkling his brow.

"Could be either. But a raven preying on another bird seems more like a bad omen to me."

Mr. H went back to writing on a notepad. Chester and Kito trotted to the shore for a sip of water. On the dock, Mrs. Hollinghorst was at her easel, painting. Her dragonfly smock fluttered in the light breeze.

Nearby, lying on their stomachs at the end of the dock, were the two new neighbor girls. The whole Tweet family was red-headed as Irish setters.

"No, Emmaline!" said Zoey, who was ten. "Don't try to catch a dock spider—they're hairy and gross! Play with Chester and Kito instead!"

Emmaline, two years younger, frowned. Her curly hair looked ratty and in need of a brushing. "But Mom would love to see a dock spider," she said. "They're cute and fuzzy. She could use one in her collection, maybe write about them for *National Geographic*."

Kito looked from the girls to the water, still thinking about the raven. "I have a bad feeling." He lapped his fill of lakewater, then heard the rustle of something nearby.

In the hollowed trunk of a cedar tree, a gray squirrel busily stuffed its treasure. Then it darted off and the dogs left the girls and Mrs. H behind. They chased the squirrel through leaves of gold, crimson, and rust.

When the squirrel ran across Pine Street toward the weathered, gray church, Kito and Chester stopped. The church, with its mossy roof and square tower, had stood vacant for years. Only two weeks ago, the Tweet family had moved in: two girls, a mom and dad, and one mean charcoal cat named Sheeba. Kito had met her—claws to nose—and didn't care to encounter her again. He scanned the neighbor's weedy yard for any sign of movement. Nothing—only the creaking of a glider from the empty swing set outside, and the sound of pounding hammers and buzzing saws from within the old clapboard church walls. From the church's square turret, yellow eyes peered down at them, then disappeared.

2

Missing Dogs!

Kito's ears perked up. Above the din next door, the sound of friendly bicycle tires rolled along the street. Sure enough, promptly on schedule, Howie Duncan, the newspaper carrier, rode toward them on his fat-tired bike. With his sack of newspapers angled across his chest, Howie was a boy in a man's body and built square as a fish cooler. He wore a tattered T-shirt and a fur-edged bomber hat strapped under his chin.

"Hi! Hi! Hi!" he called, braking to a stop.

Kito and Chester wagged their tails.

Chester sniffed. "He always smells like fish."

"Hey," Kito said, "if you ran a minnow and bait shop, you'd smell fishy too."

"Yeah, but it makes my stomach growl. Did we get fed today?" Drool began to slide out of the edge of Chester's mouth.

"Jus' wait!" Howie twisted around to the wire baskets on either side of his back tire. He searched through plastic bags, then held up two dog biscuits—one red and one green. He beamed. "For you! Cuz you're good!"

He tossed a biscuit to Chester, who missed it, then snuffled around for it on the gravel driveway.

Expertly, Kito snatched his treat midair.

Howie pushed down on his bike pedal, tottered forward, then dropped both feet down again.

"Almost fo'got." He pulled a newspaper from his canvas carrier and threw it. The paper landed halfway between the road and the front doorstep. Then he was off.

Kito grabbed the paper with his teeth

and dashed to the lake. Chester trotted after him.

Mr. H had moved from the blanket to a deck chair, pen behind his ear, notebook on his lap. His face lit up. "Kito—good dog!"

Kito panted and wagged his tail, acting like the master-serving dog that he basically was.

"Oh, dear!" Mr. H exclaimed as he read the *Daily Journal*. "Oh, my." He called to Mrs. H, "Honey, we're going to have to keep a close eye on the dogs."

Chester looked up at Kito. "What's that supposed to mean? We're in trouble again? Too many stickers on our pages at the clerk's office?"

Kito shrugged. "Wait and see." He froze at his owner's feet, facing the back page of the newspaper. It contained nothing newsworthy, just ads. When Mr. H rustled the newspaper wide open, Kito skimmed the front-page news using his undercover reading skills. The front-page headline made his stomach twist into a terrible knot of worry.

Two Pembrook Dogs
MISSING!

"Don't leave me hanging," Mrs. H called from the dock, paintbrush poised in midair. "What were you talking about?"

Mr. H looked up again. "Oh, sorry. Two Pembrook dogs are missing—that's what."

"Two dogs missing?" Zoey asked, hopping up in her ankle-high sneakers. "Oh, no!"

Chester's forehead wrinkled. "Who? Which dogs?"

A surge of fear zipped under Kito's skin. This was something bad indeed. Only last summer Tundra, their alpha village dog, had disappeared. She'd hopped a train loaded with dog food and had caught a surprise ride south. Fortunately, someone was good enough to send her back home again on the next train heading north.

Mr. H rustled the newspaper to the next page. "It says here ..."

Two dogs from separate Pembrook homes have been reported missing since last night. One of the dogs, a tan cocker spaniel known as Missy, was allegedly let outside around seven thirty and did not return.

"It's not like her," owner Fitz Rhineback said. "I go to bed early and always put her out at the same time each evening. She does her thing, then comes right in again. This has me so worried."

The other dog, known as Muffin, is owned by Thelma Jakowski. "Muffin is a fluffy little dog who loves to go for rides in the bike basket. She's friendly with everyone, and her being gone worries me no end," said Jakowski.

Kito huffed. This was bad. Muffin and Missy. They were friends and often hung out together, often lingering outside Grandma's Pantry for bits of caramel rolls every morning. If he had to bet, he'd say they likely started off on their own adventure and would be home soon. Probably there was nothing to worry about—yet.

But reason didn't help. He thought of the bad omen of the raven and its peculiar behavior. Something wrong was in the air. "Dog Watch," he said, standing tall.

Chester's tail pointed at attention. "Roger that. To the fire hydrant!"

3

The Royal Dogs
of Pembrook

The moment they veered left onto Pine Street, a shadow streaked toward them. It screeched and howled and hissed and came at them like a sidewinder snake, its body arcing and rolling.

"Sheeba!" the dogs yelped.

Fast as a greyhound, Kito bolted toward the community building. Chester bayed in fear after him. They stopped at a telephone pole, breathless, and looked back.

Head high, Sheeba was slowly tracing the edges of her new yard. Then she scaled a birch tree, settled on a branch, and glared at them with eerily green eyes.

"Another bad omen?" Chester said, catching his breath. "Isn't there s-something about black cats being bad?"

"Superstition," Kito replied. "But she's dark gray, and that's close enough for me. A bad omen that could linger around for years."

Chester stepped closer. "You're scared of her, aren't you?"

Kito winced. "Nah, she's nothing.... It's just me. My nose still smarts from last week's friendly little encounter. She'd claw our eyes out if she got the chance."

"I don't get it. We haven't done diddly to her. Why does she need to be so darn uppity with her whiskers in the air?"

13

"We're dogs," Kito replied. He stared back at Sheeba in her perch.

"Well, yeah, there's that. But we've never chased her."

"Doesn't matter. She doesn't like dogs."

"Huh. Go figure."

They turned away and trotted past the blue-trimmed community building to the post office. Usually the hydrant sat alone late in the day. Dogs lingered in the morning hours when their owners stopped to get their mail and visit with each other. After that, the dogs' lives were rarely their own.

So far, only three dogs clustered at the hydrant: Schmitty, a black Lab; Lucky, a golden retriever who would always be short one back leg; and Tundra, a white German shepherd, their alpha dog. She was sporting a red bandanna around her neck. "Big news," Tundra called. "Missy and Muffin have disappeared!"

"We heard," Kito said. "I could feel it in my fur that something was wrong. We dropped by to see if anyone knows more."

"So what's the low-down?" Chester asked, circling and sniffing the hydrant. "What else do we know at this point?"

Schmitty piped up, "That's it."

Lucky explained. "Mavis just stepped out from the post office, mumbled the headline, then went back in. That's all we know."

Tundra took charge. "Let's round-up, head to the grocery store, and see if there's any more talk."

They all trotted toward Erickson's Very Fine Grocery Store on the edge of the bay. "Dog Watch," Kito said, talking more to himself than the others, "is something we must never let die out. It's like the knights of old who defended palaces and princesses."

Schmitty raised his dark brow. "Pembrook is home, but it isn't exactly a castle."

Chester added, "And we're not exactly knights."

Tundra snorted. "And I'm not exactly a princess. By the way, where do you learn all this stuff about knights and palaces, Kito?"

"The History Channel," he replied, looking

down at the sidewalk. He didn't like her tone, exactly. More and more, he sensed she felt threatened by him. She didn't have to worry. He never wanted to be alpha.

"We watch it all the time," Chester added. "It's Mr. H's favorite."

Kito didn't want to say that after everyone fell asleep, he pawed books off the bookcase's lower shelves and read by firelight. He especially loved the stories about King Arthur and his court, carefully turning pages with the tip of his tongue and returning the books to the shelf before the fire went out.

Chester puffed out his chest. "For your information," he said, "I come from a bit of English royalty myself. Did I ever tell you that beagles were one of Queen Elizabeth's favorite breeds?"

"Uh, let me see," Lucky said. "A thousand times?"

Kito jumped back into the conversation. "But as I was saying, the knights used their physical strength and their wits toward good and toward rescuing fair maidens and—"

"Fair maidens?" Lucky interrupted. "You mean, Muffin and Missy?"

"Exactly, Lucky." He was trying to steer them toward a higher good, a mission, a sense of calling and purpose. "When you think about it," he continued, "that's really what the dogs of Pembrook do, isn't it?"

"What?" Schmitty said.

"Use our strength and wits toward good— sort of the Royal Dogs of Pembrook. And we have our queen, too."

Tundra closed her eyes in contented agreement.

"To right village wrongs—seek justice. Like King Arthur's Knights of the Round Table, let's put our noses together in a circle," Kito went on.

The dogs circled and touched noses.

Gunnar, the basset hound, trotted up and joined their circle.

"Now," Kito said, "we need a motto." He glanced at Tundra. "I mean, what do you think—should we have a motto?" Ever since she'd disappeared for those days last summer and he'd taken charge in her absence, things had never quite returned to normal. Still, he had to step back when he found himself taking charge in the alpha's presence.

"Righto," Chester said. "How about 'Morning or night, dogs take flight'?"

Tundra snorted. "Take flight? That means you're either sprouting feathers or running away. We're Pembrook dogs, not chickens!"

Kito had it. "How about 'Morning or night, Pembrook dogs unite!'?"

Lucky, Schmitty, and Gunnar started to repeat the words together, but Gunnar had a hard time keeping up. Still, the dogs all joined in unison until their voices turned to yips and barking.

Morning or night
Pembrook dogs unite!
Morning or night
Pembrook dogs unite!

Just then, Kathy stormed out of Grandma's Pantry with a broom in both hands. She knew everyone's name in the village—dogs included. "Lucky! Gunnar! Schmitty! Tundra! Kito! Chester! That's enough of your racket. Break it up. We don't need dogfights in Pembrook. Move on—you'll scare away customers." Then she turned on her heel and headed back inside. The smells of French toast, sausage, bacon, and cinnamon rolls wafted out.

"Oh, that maaaakes meeeee sooooo hungry," said Gunnar, staring at the door.

"Hey, better yet—I smell beef scraps!" Chester cried.

At the corner grocery store, Mr. Erickson had just stepped out of the back door with a cardboard box of butcher scraps. Chester took off baying, with Gunnar, Schmitty, and Lucky right behind.

Kito sighed heavily. "So much for knights in shining armor," he said to Tundra. "Two of the village dogs are missing, and all they think about is food!"

"This is true," Tundra said. "But right now, a quick snack wouldn't hurt anyone. Besides, we need to keep up our energy for what might be ahead."

Kito's mouth watered. Tundra was right.

4

The Poster

Kito lifted his head from his paws. He'd settled with the other dogs for a quick afternoon nap outside the store. He woke to voices and needed to pay attention. The grocery store door opened.

"I wouldn't be surprised if both dogs show up soon," Mr. Erickson said from the open doorway. "Your Muffin's a smart little dog, and I bet she and Missy are out on an adventure."

Thelma Jakowski, Muffin's owner, stepped over Chester and put her grocery bag in the front basket of her bicycle—where Muffin had always ridden. Dry leaves blew across Kito's snout, but he didn't let that distract him. He was back on duty.

"Too much of an adventure," said Thelma, her voice wavering. "I'm worried to death. One day she's here and the next—gone. Please, if you hear anything, Mr. Erickson, please call."

"Of course, I'll let you know."

"Last I saw little Muffin," she said sadly, "she was heading toward the ice rink."

And then she biked away.

"Hey, dogs!" Chester sat up sharply, his floppy ears cuffed in alertness. "Did ya catch that? Muffin—she was last seen—"

Schmitty, Gunnar, and Lucky hadn't. They were still sleeping.

"Sure did," Kito said.

Mr. Erickson stared off toward Grandma's Pantry, the railroad crossing, and the post office beyond. He crossed his arms over his stained white apron. "Strange," he said to himself. "One dog, I can understand.

But two at once—that's worrisome." Then, as if remembering when his own dog had disappeared months earlier, he said, "Tundra—come here, girl."

Tundra stretched out her front legs, then brushed against Mr. Erickson and leaned into his legs while he scratched her neck.

"Get up, guys," Kito said. "Attention!"

The other dogs opened their eyes, scrambled to their paws, and stood idly by as Tundra watched them like a queen observing her knights.

"That's my girl," said Mr. Erickson. "Now, you stick around, y'hear? Stay close, I don't want to lose you again."

In the store window, taped between Halloween decorations of pumpkins, bats, and ghosts, was a "Missing" poster. The photo of Muffin showed her sitting, paws up, with her curly black-and-white coat. She must have been begging. And Missy's photo must have been taken right after she'd been groomed. Rather than her usually rumpled coat, her cocker spaniel fur flowed like waves of caramel around her short and stocky frame.

Kito shot Tundra a meaningful look. "We're heading to the ice rink," he said.

"Good," Tundra agreed. "I'll listen for any more news here at the shop. Looks like I need to stick around. Meet back when you can." She sat on her haunches, her eyes sharp and ready for anything. "Dog Watch," she said, "is on full alert. Code Orange."

"What's Code Orange?" asked Lucky under her breath.

"Beats me," said Chester.

"It sounds veeery serious!" Gunnar added.

"And," Tundra added with a nod of her head, "when I'm not with the rest of you, Kito's in charge."

5

Free to a Good Home

As the dogs headed down Main Street, they approached the red, white, and blue flag fluttering above the post office. And there on the entrance steps to the Pembrook post office—to Kito's surprise—sat a big cardboard box with a sign:

FREE TO A GOOD HOME—
Talk with Bud

No one was outside the post office. The dogs approached the box gingerly, keeping a safe distance.

"What in the canine world?" Chester crept toward the box, then jumped back again.

"Don't be such a scaredy-dog," Schmitty said, padding closer. The rest of the dogs followed his lead.

When whimpering erupted from the box, the dogs fell back. Kito trembled, then stepped forward, back hairs up, and looked inside.

"Puppies!" he said. "Why haven't we heard about this litter?"

Now the four puppies started jumping around, stretching their heads to the top edge of the box. Their wavy coats were hues of black, amber, white, and tan—mutts, for sure. No telling what breeds they were. Their tiny mouths and little pink tongues were busy—panting, licking, gnawing on the box and each other. They whimpered and whined and sniffed the other dogs in return, and their tails thumped the walls of the box.

"Aaa-door-able," said Gunnar.

Kito, Lucky, Schmitty, and Chester smiled. The puppies were cute and cuddly. "Smell liiike trouble tooo meee."

"Maybe they're not from here," Schmitty said, as one puppy licked his nose. "Cute little fellas. Bet someone from out of town figured this being such a dog-friendly place, they'd find a home here."

"With two dogs missing," Kito said, "who would leave puppies out here?" Kito's sense of danger kicked in. With the news that Muffin was last seen headed to the rink, they needed to investigate, but they couldn't leave these pups unguarded. "Hey, if we start barking, maybe the owner will come back."

"Yeah, I hope they find good homes," said Chester. He let a puppy nibble at his ear.

Kito read the sign again. "Like the sign here says—" He stopped short. Almost gave himself away! He'd have to be more mindful.

"Like the sign says—what?" Chester asked. His forehead wrinkled in question.

"Oh, like the sign probably says. On TV, I've heard it more than once about dogs in need of good homes. Well, cats, too—but we don't really care about cats, do we?"

Schmitty shook his head. "Not me—they'd make for a good chase, but that's about all."

Lucky shifted her weight but settled again on her three legs. "Well, Butterball—I have to admit that, well, she snuggles up next to me at night."

Chester snorted. "Where's your doggone dignity? We know you have to share your home with a cat, but your bed, too?"

"When I was recovering from my accident, she was always there checking in on me. I came to actually enjoy her purring. I mean, she's sweet and—"

"Hold the doggone phone," Chester said. "We have a killer cat across the street from us who would just as soon eat these puppies here if she could. Don't get all sentimental about cats on us, Lucky."

"Enough, guys," Kito said. "Cats—and even these puppies here—are the least of our worries right now. We need to figure out what happened to Missy and Muffin and get them back, ASAP."

"Whaaaat's thaaat meeeean?" Gunnar asked.

"As soon as possible." Kito was not in a mood to waste time. "Now let's head toward the rink. That's where Thelma said she last saw Muffin heading—remember, guys? But before we go," Kito continued, planting himself beside the box of puppies, "let's draw some attention here. Maybe the owner of these puppies is at the tavern or inside the post office."

"Good thinking," Schmitty agreed. "I'll start."

Within seconds they had started barking and had created a commotion that anyone within two blocks would have trouble ignoring. And out of the post office stormed Mavis, the postmaster, and on her heels a stranger with a blue baseball cap and plaid shirt.

"What's all the racket about?" Mavis shouted, hands on her hips. "You dogs settle down. Those are nothing more than puppies and they're not going to hurt you dogs."

"She has that wrong," Chester said as the barking quieted. "We're not scared *of* them, just *for* them."

Mavis continued to speak to the dogs as if they could understand her words, which of course they could. "Bud brought his puppies from his farm. No one around his place for miles, so he's hoping to find some good homes here for this litter."

"Yeah, cats I can keep by the zillions, since they earn their keep," Bud said to Mavis, his hands palms up, as if asking for her understanding. Mavis was hardly the type to be romanced, but Kito had the hunch that that was what Bud was doing, in his own farmerly way. "Cats—they keep the mice and rodent population down, otherwise I'd have a disaster with all the grain and feed I have on hand for my livestock."

Kito signaled the other dogs with his eyes. Now that the owner was back out with his puppies, the dogs could move on. They trotted off as a pack.

Gunnar gave the tavern a yearning glance as they passed. "But I waaaas hoping for some leftoooover piiiiizza—"

"Pizza, schmizza!" Chester said. "You can find that anytime at the tavern. It's Muffin and Missy we should be worrying about."

"Yo, Chester," Schmitty teased. "Seems you were sidetracked not long ago by Harry's beef scraps."

Kito glanced back over his shoulder. "Stop arguing and use your senses. We have work to do.

Chester stuck his nose higher in the air and trotted on.

6

The Ice Rink

Kito surveyed the village streets for strangers or signs of anything amiss. Sniffing and snuffling, Chester and Gunnar pressed their noses to the ground. Schmitty and Lucky lagged behind, debating the good and bad points of cats.

They turned left from Main onto Pine Street, took another left, and headed past houses toward the ice rink. Closed for the season, it was tucked at the base of a hill with a small building right beside it. In winter the hill and rink bustled with kids sliding and skating, shouting and laughing. It was a place dogs loved to visit.

Weeds now surrounded the simple warming house, where kids—and dogs—warmed up on frigid days. And rather than surrounding a sheet of ice, the white rink boards enclosed a field of withered brown grass. The dogs stopped at a distance, staring.

Kito hadn't been to this corner of the village all summer long. His heart fluttered. His senses told him an unmistakable truth: *Muffin had recently been here.*

Aspen leaves fluttered against a blue sky and flecked the ground in shades of yellow and gold. The railroad tracks stretched in either direction beyond the rink. No trains, no kids. Everything was strangely quiet.

"Why would Muffin have come here?" Kito asked aloud. "She went this way near bedtime—why?"

Schmitty scratched his floppy black ears with his hind leg. "Met Missy here for an adventure?"

"Maybe they hip-hopped a train," Chester

suggested. "Same as Tundra, they found a car loaded with dog food, and zippity-doo-dah—off they went." He sniffed in the direction of the tracks. "If I found a boxcar of—"

"But think about Tundra," Kito said. "Her legs."

"What?" Chester lifted his nose from the ground. "Tundra's legs? Long, a little dirty on the feet, but—"

"And Muffin and Missy," Kito continued. "No taller than you, right?"

"Hey," Chester said, standing taller, tilting his head up, overbite showing. "I'm definitely, *positively* taller than Muffin. And Missy—I guess we stand about shoulder to shoulder."

Kito looked away. "Do you think those two could jump up into a boxcar?"

Chester's brow wrinkled into tiny folds. Gunnar's worry lines drooped around his bloodshot eyes.

"No, something else happened," Kito continued. "We're going to find out before any more dogs mysteriously disappear."

If small dogs were at a greater risk, Kito thought, he had better keep a close eye on Chester, his buddy.

"Fan out," he commanded. "Follow every scent. Keep sharp! Lucky and Schmitty: You guys take the hill and surrounding woods. Gunnar: You check inside the rink."

"But… thaaaat wooon't taaaake long."

"Not to see if she's there. Use your super smeller nose for clues."

"Ohhhh. Riiiiight."

"Chester, you and I will search the rink's perimeter and along the tracks."

Chester cleared his throat. "There you go, using those big words again. Uh, 'perimeter'?"

"Means the distance around something. In this case, I mean the outside of the rink."

"Yeah—got it," Chester said. "That's language I understand."

"And our motto?"

They pressed their noses together—Kito, Chester, Lucky, Schmitty, and Gunnar—and recited, "Morning or night, Pembrook dogs unite!"

Then they darted off.

Chester huffed and put his nose to the ground, doing what he did best. *Snuffle, snuffle, snuffle.* He plowed through piles of fallen leaves that the wind had pushed along the rink boards. Head buried to his shoulders, Chester threw leaves, rooting like a wild boar.

Slowly walking the perimeter, Kito looked for anything unusual—the shape of a stranger escaping, someone whose stance or stride was not familiar. He stumbled over lost hockey pucks and discarded pop cans, but didn't find anything that resembled a clue. He was checking under a bush when a sound floated on the air and grabbed his attention. *Awoo-wooooooo!*

A thin, high cry, a dog's whine—or song … He jumped. The voice was a dog's, no doubt about it, and he could barely hear it. There it was again. *Awoo-wooooooo!*

"Chester, did you hear that?"

Chester lifted his snout, a damp leaf stuck to the tip of his black nose. His floppy ears perked. "What?"

"Shhh." Again the sound floated toward them, just barely audible.

Awoo-wooooooo!

"Where's it coming from?" Chester snapped his head left, then right. "I can't tell."

"That's Muffin!" Kito said. He studied the woods beyond the tracks, the sliding hill and surrounding thicket, and the warming house. He strained to hear the cry one more time so he could go after it, but just then a train began rumbling through the village, shaking the ground and growing louder. *Shoosh! Shoosh! Shoosh!* The train engine's horn blew—*Wonnnnnnk! Wonk! Wonk!!*—announcing its departure from the village.

"Can't hear anything now!" Chester called. He motioned to the boarded-up building. "Maybe she's locked in there!" They ran toward the warming house. Schmitty met them coming around the corner.

"Did y'hear?" Chester barked, colliding head-on with Schmitty.

Schmitty gave him a curious look. "Uh, no. What?"

"Muffin!" said Kito. "Soft and faint, but we both heard her. Singing one of her melancholy country songs—at least that's what it sounded like to me."

Schmitty cocked his head. "Sure? I've been circling the warming house and haven't heard a thing."

"Sure as dog chews," Chester replied.

"Schmitty," Kito asked, nose pointed at the warming house door. "Have you tried the door?"

"I nosed it, but it's locked up tight."

"The window?" Kito offered. "Chester could stand on your back and peer in."

"My *back*?" Schmitty looked disgusted at the thought. "Oh, all right. I suppose Muffin could be locked inside."

Bred to handle duck hunting and frigid temperatures, built sturdy and strong, Schmitty squared his Labrador body beneath the window. Chester took a run and leaped onto his back—then promptly flew over Schmitty to the other side, and, hit the ground, rolling in somersaults. "Oooof!"

Chester lifted his head, embarrassed. "Criminy crackers! That didn't work."

In no time he jumped back on his feet, shook his coat, and tried again. He slowed his approach, gritted his teeth, and landed on Schmitty's back in perfect form.

"You could stand to lose a pound or two," Schmitty grumbled.

Kito kept watch to make sure there weren't any humans approaching. Acting too human was something the dogs tried to avoid. It would only draw attention.

"What do you see?" Kito asked.

The other dogs stopped to watch.

"Nothing," Chester groaned. "I'm not tall enough! Can't even see in the window!"

"Go ahead, jump up," Schmitty said. "I can take it."

Indeed, Chester was a practiced jumper. Kito had watched him countless times jumping straight into the air when he was waiting outside the door at home. When Kito wanted to get in, he preferred barking or scratching. Not Chester. He jumped up and down, ears flapping like wings.

And that's what he did now.

"I"—*jump*—"can"—*jump*—"see"—*jump*—"it's"—*jump*—

"Is she there?" Schmitty asked.

"It's"—*jump*—"empty."

"Fine then," Schmitty said, stepping aside as Chester made a last leap upward.

"Oooof!" The beagle landed in a tumble where Schmitty had been standing.

"But we heard her," Kito said. Again that weird feeling came over him. It was the week of Halloween, and maybe that made him extra jumpy, but the worst kind of thought came to him. "If she's not in the warming house," he said, looking gravely around at the others, "then ..."

"Yes?" Lucky said.

Schmitty pressed closer. "Then *what*?"

Kito glanced at the empty rink and silent warming house. "What if we heard Muffin—but it wasn't really Muffin?"

"Kito, please," Lucky said.

"Saaaay what yoooou mean," Gunnar pleaded.

Kito shook his coat, as if to free himself from a chilling possibility. "I mean—what if we heard Muffin's ... *ghost*?"

Poof!

At the word "ghost," the dogs turned on their padded paws and took off. Kito didn't bother to look back until he reached the stop sign at Main and Pine, even though he had the distinct sense of being followed.

The other dogs paused too.

Kito glanced back. To his relief, it was only Gunnar, loping behind them, trying to catch up with the rest. His sides heaved in and out. "Did you reeeeeally heeeeear a ghooooost?"

Kito blinked. He didn't know what to think. "I don't know, Gunnar. Sure sounded

43

like Muffin. The sound was everywhere—," he began.

"And nowhere," Chester butted in. "And when have we ever had trouble following a dog's voice before?"

The dogs looked at one another.

"Never," Schmitty, Lucky, and Gunnar said at once.

"It was a ghost," Chester said. "Sure as dog food."

Kito started off toward the post office. "Something's going on down there. C'mon, follow me."

The dogs set off after him, barking.

Outside the post office, on the bottom step, sat Bud. His head was bowed and on his knees he held the cardboard box. Mavis stood behind him, patting his shoulder.

The dogs drew closer.

"... I get to talkin'," Bud said, "and I s'pose it could have been longer than a few minutes ... but who would take all the puppies without asking me first? I mean, if the sign says 'to a good home' you'd think ..."

Mavis looked over Bud's shoulder into the box, as if to make sure the pups were truly gone. "That's *weird*, Bud. No other word for it."

Kito turned to face the other dogs. "Yes, who would just take the pups? No one would take four puppies at once as pets. That would be unheard of."

"They were just here," Schmitty said, tilting his head in bewilderment, "and—poof!—they're gone!"

Despite her missing leg, Lucky sat on her haunches. "Someone kind may have picked them all up. When I was hit by a car, the driver stopped and put me in his car, drove me all the way to the vet's for emergency help—and then called my owners."

"Yeah, but barkin' biscuits, this was no emergency," Chester said.

"Riiiiight," Gunnar agreed. "Thiiis iiiis diiifffereent."

The dogs looked up and down the street. They took turns sniffing inside Bud's empty cardboard box.

"Without a doubt," Schmitty said, "smells like puppies."

Kito paced, thinking aloud. "Odd that they didn't take the box, too. If someone was in a car and picked them up, they could be miles away by now. But why? Or did they simply vanish?" He shivered. All the old fears from his difficult puppyhood came rushing back, filling him with dread. Because of the bad treatment he'd received in his early years, he found he could never completely relax. He was always waiting for something bad to happen—some unexpected meanness to come his way for no good reason.

Mavis gave Bud one last pat on his shoulder. "Time for me to get the mail bagged and ready for pickup," she said, and the door swung shut behind her.

"Yup, and I better get back to the farm," Bud said to the dogs. "Gotta put the cows in and button things up for the night." He brushed off his coveralls and picked up his empty box with a heavy sigh. He carried it to his pickup, put it in back, then drove off slowly.

The dogs huddled near the hydrant.

"I'm feeeeelin' soooo blue," Gunnar said, his eyes looking droopier and sadder than ever, "about Miiissy and Muffiiin, and nooow the little pups. I thiiiink I better goooo...." And with that he ambled off to the tavern and squeezed inside as a customer headed out.

Kito barked. "Let's head back to tell Tundra the latest—"

"Wait." Lucky pointed her snout toward the community building across the street. The dogs followed her gaze. Mr. Cutler was stacking hay bales outside. A banner spanned the door that read: SPOOK HOUSE TONIGHT—FOR KIDS OF ALL AGES! 7:00! The windows were decorated with scarecrows, black cats, ghosts, and witches. Cobwebs stretched across every windowpane.

"If tonight's the Spook House," Kito said, "then *tomorrow* must be Halloween."

"Yeah, the scariest, creepiest night of the year," Chester said. "Enough to make a sane dog go crazy."

Kito glanced toward the bay. The sun was already dipping low over Seven Oaks Park, and it wasn't even suppertime yet. The days were growing shorter and shorter and the shadows longer and longer.

"C'mon," Kito said. "We better check in with Tundra. We're losing dogs faster than we can find them."

"Criminy!" Chester cried. "The way things are going around here, who knows what might happen on Halloween?"

Search Party

Tundra rose from her nose-and-tail-tucked-into-a-ball position and stood tall and regal as the dogs approached.

"Chester, you look like you just saw a ghost!"

"We did—I mean, we might have heard … but puppies are missing and …"

"The Spook House—it's tonight!" Lucky added.

"Slow down, slow down," Tundra said. "Tell me what you've learned."

Once she had heard them out, she sat

down firmly, her white feathery tail curled alongside her. "Here's the plan," she said. "We need to make a wider sweep of the village. Kito—you're good at organizing. You take the meeting from here."

Kito cleared his throat. "Okay, then. Listen up," he began. "Teams of two. No dog is to venture off alone. We can't be too careful right now. Chester—you and I will scout the northern loop of Pembrook Beach. Schmitty and Lucky, you guys cover the southern end, but don't get too close to the highway. We don't want any accidents."

He paused, looking each dog in the eyes. "On your way there," he continued, "stop by the tavern and tell Gunnar to check the eastern edge—he should find another buddy to work with. And drop by Willow's house— she could probably get Scooter to work the eastern portion near the bay together. Look for signs of dog-napping, of struggle, of anything that might seem unusual. Head home for dinner to keep suspicions low with your owners, then we'll all meet at the community building before the doors open to the Spook House."

Tundra stepped forward, as if to remind them who was officially in charge. "If we work together, we're bound to stumble across something," she said. "And I don't want to alarm any of you, but if we don't get to the bottom of this, other dogs might go missing as well. So be careful out there."

"And remember," Chester added, in a TV announcer tone, "the life you save may be your own."

Though Chester meant to be funny, no one laughed. Instead, his words left a disturbing chill in the air.

"Head out," said Tundra.

Kito and Chester set off on the loop past Pembrook Beach. They passed a little house alongside the railroad tracks where Spike had been chained up to a doghouse as long as they could remember. Built lean and tough as a railroad spike, he started barking in a gravelly voice—then lunged at the end of his heavy chain.

"Good thing for the chain," Kito said as they trotted past.

A true mutt—part curly hair, part straight, with long legs and a small nose—Spike had wiry hair that stuck out in tufts from his ears and curled over his back. He was barking so hard that foam frothed around the corners of his mouth.

Kito avoided eye contact with Spike, which only made the other dog angrier. He was glad for the chain. In his roaming days, Spike had wrestled more than one dog to the ground, leaving blood behind.

"What did he do?" Chester whispered as they headed down the street.

"Last one he bit was a delivery man, who had to get his leg stitched up. Spike was ordered to be chained up or put down."

"You mean, put to sleep—killed?"

"Yup. People don't take kindly to biting—and he's a *real* biter."

"Let's keep moving."

They followed the north side of the railroad tracks past the small Ric-Jig Tackle

factory, known for making fishing lures. Not a light was on. The parking lot was empty. The air around the building was always ripe with strange smells—foul scents used for tackle. But other than that, nothing seemed out of place, so they continued on.

Ahead was Howie's home, if you could call it that. It was an old mobile home tucked among a cluster of aspen trees, their branches now bare as bones. In the summer, Howie's place was completely hidden by greenery, which wasn't all bad. Now you could see everything: the rusted-out remains of three cars and a truck, piles of metal scraps and wood, a shed that was more tilted than straight, and the little wooden sign at the end of his driveway that read: MINNOWS AND LEESHES—HEAR!

Every time they passed this way, Kito wanted to joke about Howie's spelling. Of course it should read, "Minnows and Leeches—here!" but he couldn't tell Chester that.

Just then Howie came running out of his

mobile home. He hopped on his bike and pedaled full speed at them.

"Hi! Hi! Hi! Late—almost fo'got my papers. Gotta go!"

Off he biked, with his empty newspaper sack whipping across his body. Kito knew his routine. Howie always picked up his batch of daily newspapers at the grocery store before making the village rounds. He left a distinct fishy smell in his wake.

"Huh," Chester said. "I don't suppose he's selling many minnows these days."

"Nope. Hardly any boats on the lake in the fall. Summer he has people coming and going all the time, but it's pretty quiet now. Maybe business picks up when the lake freezes over and ice fishing starts up."

"Think he's always lived alone?" Chester asked.

"No, he used to live with his parents, but they both went to a nursing home a few years back—before your time."

"Hmmm. Seems sad—all alone like that, and not too smart to boot."

"All the same, I sure like Howie."

"Me too."

They trotted on, rounded the farthest end of their loop, then made their way past small cottages and large homes. When they reached Lakeview Cabins, a cluster of little cabins overlooking the lake, Chester dropped his nose deeper into the leaves and caught a whiff of something. A wind picked up, and Kito's back hairs tingled. Between Cabins Five and Six, Dr. Elizabeth Jensen was busy raking leaves into piles. Her white hair was wild, despite the polka-dot scarf she wore. In jeans, boots, and a plaid wool jacket, she paused, stood straight, and pressed her hand to her lower back. "Darn hard work, this is. Every year it's the same. I end up doing it all myself."

The dogs drifted closer, even though she was clearly not in a good mood. The cabins looked on, empty and lonely. "You dogs there—now don't start messing up my piles. I've spent all day raking."

But Chester could never resist a good

leaf pile. He aimed his snout for the nearest pile, then snuffled and snorted, snorted and snuffled his way through, plowing the leaves to his right and his left as he went.

"Chester," Kito warned. "Don't!"

"Out!" Elizabeth cried. She waved her rake like a sword. "That's enough!"

Just as she was within inches of Chester's rump, the wind picked up and blew her leaves to and fro. The tip of her bamboo rake nicked Chester's rump. "Wooooo!" he cried.

Kito barked, "Let's go!" They didn't need to be reported for causing trouble. Another round sticker on his page, along with the few he'd earned already, and he might end up like Spike—stuck in his own yard forever. He glanced over his shoulder, but the doctor had returned to her raking. Her white hair was a dim light in the growing shadows. The dogs bolted from Lakeview Cabins.

"All you do is come asking for treats—or trouble," Dr. Elizabeth called. "I could sure use some help instead!"

Kito hated to run off like that, but the way

she'd brandished her rake scared him. He raced around the street corner, then down the embankment, to Pembrook Beach for a drink.

"Four puppies," he said as he finished lapping, "and two dogs disappear without a trace. If someone liked dogs, they wouldn't steal them. So shouldn't we be looking for someone who doesn't like dogs—"

"Like Dr. Elizabeth?" Chester asked.

"Well, yes. Maybe like her. And if someone took dogs, wouldn't they need a place to hide them—like in *empty cabins*?"

Chester began prancing around nervously. "Or—or—bury them? I sure came across some strange smells in those leaf piles. Old things. Rotting things."

Across the bay on the Canadian shore, the sun was setting, leaving a trail of red across the water. Kito could barely take in Chester's words. "Sun's down. The Spook House is going to start before long."

"Didn't you hear

what I said?" Chester asked, stepping right in Kito's path, nose to his nose.

Kito let out a deep breath. "All too well, my friend. We're definitely going to return for a better look around at Dr. Elizabeth's cabins. But for now, let's head home, wolf down some dinner. We'll formulate a plan—and then we'll come back."

"Yeah, like when she's sleeping."

"You got that right."

9

Spook House

After a shared bowl of Hearty Hound at home, the dogs rushed back to the door and woofed.

"What's going on out there?" Mrs. H asked as she opened the door. "What's the rush?"

But off they raced, back on duty. Kito gave a sideways glance to the Tweets' church-home. No cat in sight. Without slowing their pace to see if Sheeba was on the hunt, they hurried to the community building.

The Spook House was ready to open. Dogs gathered outside the community building. A line of cars was parked curbside. Kids in costumes clustered at the door, which opened just as Kito and Chester arrived.

Howie rode by on his bike. Dressed up like a clown—with a tattered plaid shirt, a floppy yellow hat, and his face painted white—he smiled, red paint framing his mouth with an extra huge smile.

"Hi! Hi! Hi! Hal'ween party!" he called, bumping over the curb across the grassy lawn. He hopped off his bike and let it thump to the ground behind him, and then headed inside.

"Time to go!" Chester called. "Where there's a party, there are bound to be treats!"

And with that, Chester headed through the door as it opened behind Howie. Kito slipped in right behind and reminded his buddy, "Treats are fine and good, but remember, we're still looking for clues. Don't forget about Missy and Muffin and those little puppies—not for a second."

"Got it."

The wood-floored room was a swirl of costumes, noise, and decorations. It was hardly the same place where the mayor and council met every Monday.

Kids and adults played games, laughed, ate, and talked. On the right side of the small stage hung a black curtain with a sign above: SPOOK HOUSE: ENTER AT YOUR OWN RISK! Kids were lined up, waiting.

A shower of water suddenly hit Kito's back. He spun around. Behind him, a teenage boy was shaking water from his hair as another boy bobbed for apples in a barrel.

"C'mon, Austin! Try again!" two boys cheered. From head to toe they were dressed in black, and their faces were painted in red and black stripes. Kito bristled. He wasn't sure he had ever seen these teenagers before. Were *they* up to no good as far as dogs were concerned?

One of the boys noticed Kito. "Hey, sorry we got you wet!"

With a quick shake of his coat, Kito headed

to the treat table. Maybe he'd misjudged them. A black cauldron of apple cider sat on one end, followed by bowls of popcorn and roasted pumpkin seeds, and plates loaded with frosted pumpkin and black cat cookies. Kito ducked under the tablecloth to check for crumbs, then tensed.

To his surprise, Howie was under the table, too! He crouched with his arms around his knees, sniffling and his clown makeup ran down his face.

At times like this, Kito wished he could ask aloud, "What's wrong?" But speaking was beyond him. He nudged Howie's knee, and Howie patted the top of Kito's head in return.

"I'm weally scared," Howie said, whimpering. "So scared—monsters."

Kito wagged his tail and licked Howie's face until he smiled.

"You scared too?"

And that was all it took. Howie crawled out after Kito and looked around the room.

Kito felt a shiver of worry—there were some creepy costumes, and so real looking!

A green-faced monster helped three kids with the Bean Bag Toss. A mummy wrapped in strips of tattered gray cloth moved slowly through the crowd, moaning and dragging one leg. Dracula helped kids carve pumpkins. A black-hatted witch with a long, warty nose emerged from the kitchen. In her hands she carried two jugs of cider, which she poured into the cauldron. Next she dropped in something that made clouds of white spill from the pot. "Hee, hee, hee!"

she cackled, then returned to the kitchen.

No wonder Howie was scared! Not only were some of the costumes frightening, but from behind the Spook House curtain came shrieks, screams, laughs, and ghostlike cries.

Several dogs wandered among the kids, hoping for a dropped cookie or spilled popcorn. Kito caught a glimpse of Gunnar and Chester, talking beside a scarecrow sitting on a hay bale. Kito edged closer.

"I'm telllin' youuuu," Gunnar said. "Schmitty wennnnnt in and heeee hasn't come ouuuut."

"Where?" Kiko interrupted. "The Spook House?"

"Yup—not gooooood."

"Kito," Chester said. "You and I. We're right on it, aren't we?"

Kito glanced at the black curtain, and listened to a new series of wails and moans coming from behind the curtained stage. His legs trembled. It would be dark in there, with so many things he couldn't see. Did he really want to risk going in after Schmitty? Absolutely not.

"How long has he been in there?" Chester asked.

"Ohhh, a long tiiiime."

Chester's tail went straight out. He lifted his right foot into a "point" position. "That's it! We're going in."

Kito could tell he had no choice. Reluctantly, he followed Chester to the line of kids standing behind the curtained door that Mr. Cutler guarded.

At the front of the line they found Emmaline, hopping up and down in butterfly wings of orange and gold. Her older sister, Zoey, was dressed up in a white doctor's coat with a stethoscope around her neck. Written on her chest pocket was the word "Vet."

"I'm scared," Emmaline told her.

"Don't worry. If you can catch big spiders, you can handle the Spook House."

Behind them the line was made up of a cowboy, a wizard, a robot, a dragon, a fire-fighter, a ghost, and a hobbit—all waiting their turns.

"You two are next," said Mr. Cutler, holding the curtain aside as the butterfly and vet stepped in.

As they did, Kito and Chester scooted in after them.

"Hey! No dogs!" Mr. Cutler shouted.

But they'd already slipped past the curtain and into the utter darkness.

10

Spook House Spook!

Once they passed through the curtain, screams and howls and blackness engulfed them. A shiver of terror ran through Kito's four legs. A hand slipped through his collar and held fast. He didn't blame Emmaline or Zoey for being scared. They needed someone to help protect them. Besides, having one of them near helped ease his own fears. He didn't mind one bit.

"Which way do we go?" asked Emmaline.

"I don't know!" said Zoey. "I can't see anything!"

Kito felt himself tugged and nudged, and the hand on his collar held fast as he moved forward.

"Kito," Chester said from somewhere ahead. "Are you there?"

"Yeah, behind you—just a few steps."

"Good. This place gives me the willy wigglies!"

A dim purplish light glowed ahead. In a cluster, the little group stepped toward it. The light flooded a long and low rectangular box. The coffin lid was open, and as they drew closer a white hand reached up and gripped the edge. An old man with stringy gray hair sat up, ever so slowly, moaning.

Chester started howling.

The girls screamed.

Kito barked, but the hand on his collar pulled harder, cutting off his voice.

Off they ran around the nearest corner and plunged into the dark maze again.

Suddenly, a beam of light shone on a pile of rags.

Chester stepped up to it, sniffing. "Somebody's garbage, or—"

The pile of rags shifted, and a hand reached out for Chester. Wrapped from head to foot, the mummy stood tall and roared. It rattled the broken chains attached to its arms.

The girls screamed and took off, and Kito was pulled after them again. He thought he had caught the scent of someone very familiar—Mr. Hollinghorst? Was his owner dressed up like a mummy? He didn't have time to give it another sniff, because suddenly, an ear-splitting cackle filled the stuffy air. Between two small pine trees, a witch was hunched over her pot. She stirred and laughed wickedly. Startled, she glanced over her shoulder and looked straight at them.

"Oh, dear guests! Just what I need for my special brew! I'll cook and stir, then chew and chew!" She cackled again and reached her long, bony fingers at them, and they all took off again—with Chester's howls louder than the girls' shrieks.

Kito bared his teeth, ready to bite—but the tug on his collar sent him flying after the others. He wanted to go home! This was too much for a dog bred to protect and defend. It set his insides swirling and his head in a daze. He wanted to defend—how could he not? But if he bit someone …

They passed through more scares. A black cat arching its back and hissing … but on closer inspection, Kito noticed an electrical cord.

"Hey, it's a fake," he said with relief.

"Sheeba is enough of a scare," Chester whispered.

They wound their way beneath cobwebs and flashing lights, over a tiny bridge with troll hands grabbing at their feet, past Dracula with frightfully long fangs, and under a flock of ghosts floating overhead….

Kito lagged behind, as the hand still held fast to his collar. Whichever girl was holding it, she had to be scared. *He* was! So he didn't mind keeping his pace slow and staying with her for comfort.

Ahead, down a ramp, a small light illuminated a door with a tiny sign—no bigger than a dog bone. Emmaline was standing right under it. "'Enter at Your Own Risk,'" she read. Her voice trembled. "I don't know … I'm too scared! What if it's something really, really, really scary this time?"

"Just go," said Zoey from beside Kito.

Emmaline patted Chester, then pushed her butterfly shoulders back. She grabbed the door handle and turned it.

As the door cracked open, Chester bounded ahead.

Kito paused at the door's threshold and looked out. There on the grassy lawn of the community building were Chester, Emmaline in her wings, and Zoey in her vet jacket. The girls were laughing, and Chester ran in circles, wagging his tail and jumping up playfully. Beyond, Schmitty wrestled with Gunnar.

A chill settled in Kito's jaws. If Zoey and Emmaline were already outside on the lawn, then *who* was holding his collar?

The hand still held him fast—kept him

from leaving! Utter panic swept through him. He growled and pulled away with all his might from the grip that held him—*had* held him all the way through the spook house, always walking just a few steps behind his view.

He barreled forward, broke free, and tumbled out and onto the cool, grassy lawn.

"Hey, Kito!" Chester yelled. "Wasn't that fun? C'mon! Let's do it again!"

Kito glanced back. The side door of the community building was now closed. A brave dog would go back, would sniff around and explore for clues. But Kito was beyond that. Without an explanation, he bolted on trembling legs for the safety of home.

11

Strange Happenings Next Door

All night Kito tossed and turned with nightmares of the Spook House. He woke up twice with his legs running, even though he was lying on his side. Late in the morning, he startled awake with Chester standing over him, his overbite showing.

"Give a dog a heart attack, why don't you?" Kito said. "After last night, I don't need any more surprises."

"It's them—I know it."

"Them? What—who—are you talking about?"

"'Bout time you woke up. I've been up since the coffeepot was turned on. Couldn't sleep any longer. The new neighbors, that's who. The Tweet family."

"Why? What have you got?"

"Well, they seem sweet enough, but I think that family has brought nothing but trouble. Come with me, I'll show you."

Reluctantly, Kito stretched, then ambled down the wood staircase and scratched at the door. Mrs. H set a log in the woodstove, then met them in her pumpkin slippers.

"Okay, boys," she said. "Out you go."

They trotted to the edge of the street and stopped. Across the road, a pickup was parked in the Tweets' driveway. Mr. Tweet's orange hair bushed out from under his "Born to Be Wild"

cap. The dogs had learned that he flew tourists into Canada with the yellow float plane he kept in the bay. Mrs. Tweet's auburn braid reached the waist of her baggy pants, and she wore wool socks and leather sandals.

"Well, see," said Mr. Tweet to the man in the truck, "we're thinking about a basement. Can we lift the whole building up and have a basement poured?"

"Basements are creepy," Chester said. "I don't know why people need them at all. I think they have something to hide!"

"Hey, *we* have a basement, but that doesn't mean the Hollinghorsts are hiding anything."

"True. But look over there—above the old garage."

What Kito saw left him speechless. Since yesterday, someone had tacked up a massive snapping turtle's shell, moose antlers, a long jawbone, and a small animal skeleton. And on the peak of the garage sat a raven. It puffed up its scraggly wings and studied them.

"Pretty weird?" Chester whispered.

"Yup, pretty weird."

"So what do you think it all means?"

"I don't quite know."

"Another omen? Signs of bad things next door?"

"Maybe. But maybe it just means that our new neighbors are strange—nothing more. I mean, those girls seem pretty normal."

"*Seem* normal and *are* normal are two different things," Chester said with a tilt of his head.

Their musings were interrupted by the roar of the truck as it backed onto the street and took off.

Arms crossed, Mr. Tweet was still talking.

"Well that's just not possible then, Critter," said Mrs. Tweet. "Too expensive."

"Iris, honey, we're going to have to stick with our original plan."

Then they turned and went back inside the church building. As they did, the two Tweet girls came running outside, laughing. When the girls spotted the dogs, they both called out.

"Hey, Kito!"

"Hi, Chester!"

But right on the girls' heels slunk Sheeba, her green eyes intent on her prey on the opposite side of the road. *Them!* She burst forward, yowling and howling, and Kito and Chester turned on their tails and raced around their house toward the water. They darted to the end of the dock.

"Cats don't like water," Kito said.

"Yeah—we'll jump if we have to," Chester agreed.

They waited, but Sheeba didn't appear. The dogs breathed more deeply.

"This is humiliating," Kito said. "Afraid of a cat."

"Yeah, and it underscores my point. Something's not right with that family, from suddenly wanting to have a basement—to hide what? I might ask—to that odd stuff tacked up on their garage, to that raven watching us, to that stupid cat."

"Hmm. And they moved in just before dogs and puppies started to disappear."

"Criminy. Think about it, Kito. Who else could it be? And what do you suppose that little skeleton is on their garage?"

Kito swallowed hard.

"A small dog?" Chester pressed.

The idea that someone would harm a little dog or puppy was too much. "Listen," Kito said. "Calm down. Keep these thoughts to yourself for now. I'm going to get something to eat, then we'll head to the fire hydrant and see what the others have found out."

After breakfast, the two headed straight for the post of fire. Gathered around the fire hydrant were a half dozen village dogs, including Schmitty, Lucky, and Gunnar. Tundra sat at a distance from them, head high.

"So, what's the lowdown?" Chester asked as they trotted up.

"Not goooooood," Gunnar said. Drool eased out of the edges of his wet mouth. "Lossssst anotheeeer dog."

Kito stopped short, right beside Tundra. "No—is it true?"

"Afraid so," she said. "Last night at the community building. Dogs were coming and going all night, and one didn't come home—Woody was just here asking if anyone had seen her."

"Her?"

"Willow."

Kito heaved a big sigh. "Oh, this is awful. Not sweet Willow. She rolls over for anybody who just says hi to her. Takes walks with strangers. But she's never disappeared before." Willow always returned home to Woody and Leanne—of Woody's Fairly Reliable Guide Service—no matter how friendly she was to others.

"Woooooody was sick with woooorry," Gunnar said. "Heeee said his wife and boys will never fooooorgive him if sheeeee's lost foooorever."

"She won't be lost forever," said Tundra, circling the group at the fire hydrant. "Dog Watch won't let that happen."

Lucky tilted her head. "But we're not any closer to finding out who's dog-napping."

Schmitty tilted his head. "Yeah, we need to get smarter. Maybe enlist the help of old Spike."

"You mean the biter?" Chester asked. "Criminy. I don't think so. He'd rather bite than help."

Tundra said, "I think Schmitty has a good suggestion."

"We wouldn't have to let Spike off his chain—or get too close," Schmitty continued, wagging his tail with increasing excitement. "Bring him a scrap or two from the grocery store in trade for asking if he's seen anything unusual. I mean, he's the only dog around who stays outside all day, every day."

"That's right," Lucky joined in.

"What about the Tweets—our new neighbors?" Chester asked. "They mighty suspicious."

But no one seemed to listen. The dogs were already heading off in their separate directions.

"I heard you," Kito said. "We'll keep an eye on them."

12

A Warning

Kito had nearly forgotten the vet appointment until Mr. H pulled up at the curb, reached behind to open the back door, and hollered, "Kito, Chester! Come on! We're late!"

With great reluctance—because he hated sitting on that cold metal slab to be poked and prodded by the vet, and because it delayed their *real* work—Kito obeyed. He jumped in the backseat, and Chester followed.

Mr. H put the car in reverse, cranked up the music, and started singing along, which was truly painful, as he couldn't carry a tune. Chester sat back. His chin quivered, and soon he pointed his snout toward the ceiling and he was sang along, too.

Kito gazed out the window. The seriousness of his own reflection made him jump. Though his furry amber coat was handsome, the black velvet of his muzzle and his dark, serious eyes made him appear tough. If only he could find the person who was stealing dogs and puppies from the village, then he'd put his tough looks to good use. But so far, they'd come up with nothing.

When the song was over, he turned to Chester. "We need to talk."

"What's stirring in your brain?"

"The dog's cry at the ice rink," Kito began. "I could have sworn it was Muffin—or Muffin's ghost—but we've heard nothing since."

"True."

"What about the tackle factory with its strange smells? Would they use—"

"Yuck. No, I don't think so." Chester shuddered.

"Dr. Elizabeth—going after us to get us

away from her leaf piles. She didn't want us around ... so that makes me wonder what she's hiding. That puts her on my suspect list."

"Mine, too."

"And last night's scare at the Spook House, with someone hanging on to my collar the whole way.... If I hadn't pulled hard and escaped, I may have been the next dog-napped victim."

Chester tilted his head. "And let's not forget our neighbors. Weird stuff tacked above the garage door. That wild cat, Sheeba—she's spooky. Maybe the dog-napping is happening right across the street."

"Yeah, right under our noses," Kito agreed. "When we get back, we go on patrol. We check out the Tweets' yard and look for signs of paw prints, struggle, anything we can find. And then we'll try to get close to Spike—see if he can tell us anything from his end of town. Everything is a possibility at this point."

The car pulled up and stopped in front of

All About Pets Veterinary Clinic. Kito took a deep breath. He was probably due for boosters on rabies, Lyme disease, and distemper. Three shots. Except for the cat next door, there was nothing he liked less.

When Chester was done with shots on the exam table, Mr. H hoisted Kito up next. The vet, a young woman with a voice as soothing as gravy, stroked his head and the top of his coat.

"Oh, you're a beautiful dog," she cooed. "Now let me look at your teeth."

Kito let her lift his lips and press around his gums.

"You might want to start brushing his teeth," she told Mr. H.

"Ha!" he said. "The day Kito gets his teeth brushed is the day he learns to brush them himself."

"Well, that's fine," she said, "but some dogs actually enjoy having their teeth brushed. You could work with him slowly at first."

"Yeah, and after teeth brushing, we'll work on reading, right?"

Kito glanced at the posters around the room—one about heartworm, another about Lyme disease, and another about feline leukemia.

The vet laughed softly. "He's healthy, so it's clear you're taking good care of him. If you don't want to brush his teeth, then keep him on dry foods as you're doing, and that will help keep his teeth clean and his gums healthy."

It was just as well. Kito didn't really want to have his teeth brushed.

"That's it. All done," she said, and offered Kito a few chunks of special dog treats. He couldn't believe it. She'd given him his shots and he hadn't even known it.

"Your dogs are physically fit," she said. "See you next year."

On the way out, Mr. H bought two leather dog bones and two stuffed toys—a hedgehog and a chicken. The vet stopped him before leaving. "Oh, and one more thing. By now I'm sure you're aware that several dogs have disappeared from Pembrook."

"Sure am. It's worrisome."

"Keep an eye on your dogs. I'd hate to see anything happen to them."

"That's for sure. I hope the police figure this out soon."

On the drive home, Kito and Chester took a break from Dog Watch and play-wrestled in the backseat over the stuffed toys.

"I get the hedgehog," Chester said.

"Nope. The chicken suits you better," Kito said as he tugged it away.

They were so distracted by the new toys and bones that they followed Mr. H right into the house, wrestled and chewed and hid and chased, wore themselves out, and napped away most of the afternoon.

Kito woke to the sound of Howie's singing outside. He rose from the couch, whined at the door, and with Chester at his heels, headed out to greet Howie on his bike. Kito wanted to and check out the latest newspaper headline. He'd wasted too much precious time and needed to get back on the job.

13

Trespassing

"Hi! Hi! Hi!" hollered Howie. "Happy Hal'ween!"

The dogs wagged their tails as Howie straddled his bike and pulled the *Daily Journal* from his shoulder pouch. He tossed it, and the paper landed squarely at Kito's paws. He glanced down at the headline:

More Pembrook Dogs Disappear

"M-m-m-oooo—," Howie said, shaking his head sadly. "I can't read very good."

The dogs kept wagging their tails.

"Almost fo'got," he said. He twisted around, reached into one of the plastic bags in one of his bike baskets, and tossed dog biscuits. The dogs caught them before they touched the gravel driveway.

"Bye, bye!" And off Howie went on his bike, tossing newspapers at doorsteps.

Kito scanned the front-page article. The local sheriff was quoted as saying, "We're encouraging owners to keep their dogs close to home until we get to the bottom of this."

Kito picked the paper up in his mouth, dropped it on the front doormat, then turned to Chester. "C'mon. We better get going." What he didn't say was that if Mr. and Mrs. H read the article, they might keep their dogs at home. And they couldn't afford that now. Let the police do their work, but in the meantime, Dog Watch would be at work too.

Boldly, Kito marched straight for the old church building. No one was outside, and he didn't spot Sheeba lurking in the shadows or the overgrown weeds. He glanced at the snapping turtle shell and the small skeleton above the garage door, shuddered, and kept going. Chester snorted after him, nose to the ground.

"Careful you don't inhale evidence," Kito said. Joking always helped ease his own fears.

"Hey, my nose is invaluable and you know it."

"If I see that cat, I'll bark once and we'll get out of here."

"Deal."

"Maybe the Tweets eat what they can find, like … dogs and such."

Kito turned on Chester. "Don't say that. It's too terrible. But come to think of it, people in some countries do eat dogs."

"Yeah, and I heard that the Tweets moved here after living somewhere far away."

That nervous feeling began to buzz inside Kito as he neared the side of the church building. Mr. H said the building was once used as a real church, but then it sat vacant for so long that it was scheduled to be torn down, until the Tweet family decided to make it their home. He'd said it as if it were a happy thing, but it just made Kito anxious.

They went around back and sniffed their way under a hedge of sumac bushes. The side windows of the church were open. Suddenly, Mrs. Tweet appeared at the window with binoculars and pointed. "There! Do you see it?"

The dogs ducked low, flat on their bellies.

In a second, Mrs. Tweet came flying out the door, holding high a mesh net on a skinny pole. Emmaline and Zoey marched behind her. "The spotted leopard monarch!" called Mrs. Tweet. "See it now, girls?"

She was just about to step on Kito and Chester when her net whooshed through branches overhead. "Got it! Let's get this one pinned and pressed."

"Mom," said Emmaline. "This one's perfect!"

When the door eased shut again, Kito let out his breath. "That was close," he said.

But something else had stepped outside

and was stalking them. Step by step, slowly and silently. Kito sensed that they were being followed.

Sheeba! Low to the ground, in a whining, growling, howling thundercloud, she came flying at them, her claws razor sharp and flexed.

Tails pressed between their legs, Kito and Chester fled.

14

Trick or Treat

Out of breath, and disgusted with himself for acting like a timid mouse, Kito pressed himself against the front door. From across the steeet, Sheeba glared at him and Chester.

"She's d-d-disgusting," Chester said.

"Cats are supposed to run from dogs," Kito said, "not the other way around."

Just then the door opened, and Kito nearly fell headfirst inside. "Well, what's this? You two see a ghost?" asked Mrs. H, flipping her ponytail over the shoulder of her paint-splattered workshirt. "I was looking for both of you. I need some measurements."

"Measurements?" Kito repeated.

Chester snorted with a laugh. "Yeah, for our coffins. Why worry about dog-napping? That cat's going to be the death of us."

"You two are going to love your Halloween costumes. Royal dogs, now what do you think about that?"

Chester and Kito exchanged glances.

"What's she talking about?" Chester asked.

Kito shrugged. "I'm sure we'll find out soon enough."

In seconds Mrs. H whipped purple velvet capes trimmed in fake white fur from her sewing machine. "Let's see—this one is for you, Kito," she said, holding up the larger of the two. "And this one is for you, Chester. The neighbor girls, Emmaline and Zoey, asked if you two could join them trick-or-treating tonight, so I thought, why can't dogs dress up too?" She chuckled as she fastened the capes around their necks and stood back admiringly, arms crossed. "Yes, you're both perfect." Then she burst out laughing.

Chester tried to pull his cape off with his teeth. Soon he was tripping over it and it hung around his neck like a bib.

"Just what I was afraid of," said Mrs. H. She removed the capes. "I'll have to add elastic belly straps so you can't get these off."

"Great," Kito said. "Now look what you did. We might have been able to slip them off, but now we'll be stuck wearing those silly things all night."

He followed Chester to the water and food bowls.

"My real worry," Chester said, "isn't the capes—it's shaking off those girls. I mean, what kind of child cheers when her mother is going to pin a butterfly? A strange child, that's what I say. Maybe if we act sick we won't have to go trick-or-treating with them at all."

Kito touched his nose to Chester's. "We'll go. Your nose is wet and cool—perfectly healthy. We won't have a choice."

Before the sun was down, neighborhood kids in costumes began arriving at the door. *Ding-dong! Ding-dong!*

"Trick or treat!" they shouted. Mr. and Mrs. H beamed as they dropped candy into bags and buckets. Then off the children raced in packs or toddled along with their parents.

"I wish we could figure out how to do that," Chester said. "I mean, just go to the door, ring the bell, and get fed. Think we could manage it?"

"Huh. You'd manage to get a sticker on your page—and lose your freedom, that's what."

When Emmaline and Zoey showed up as a butterfly and a vet at the door, Mrs. H bustled to the table and grabbed the dogs' costumes. "Here you go, my royal dogs!"

Kito grimaced inside as she fastened the purple cloak under his belly and around his neck.

"You look royally dorky," Chester told him. "But maybe these fancy capes will bring us a bit of luck."

"We could use some." Kito remembered the hand that had held him fast in the Spook House. If only he could figure out who it had been … whoever had tried to steal him was still out there. And Pembrook dogs and puppies were still missing!

"They're so cute!" Emmaline and Zoey cried as the dogs rounded the corner.

"Kito and Chester," Mrs. H said. "You two stay with the girls, okay?" Then she did something unexpected. She took out their little-used leashes and clipped one to each of their collars. "This way I know you'll stay at their sides. Now you protect Emmaline, Chester. And Kito, you take care of Zoey. You're my royal dogs."

"Royal dogs of Pembrook!" Chester added as they headed out. "At least I'm AKC registered."

With a cautious glance toward the neighbors, Kito stepped outside. No sign of Sheeba, so he continued on quietly, tail down. He felt a yank on his neck and glanced back at Zoey in her vet costume. "Don't pull so hard," she said. "You're hurting my hand. Walk nice, please."

Her voice was gentle, not scary. He slowed down and walked with her from house to house. At every doorstep, people exclaimed, "Oh, you girls are adorable. And look at the dogs—they are too!"

Kito just felt stupid. But cape or no cape, he would take his job seriously. He and Chester would help protect these girls, and while they were doing that, they would try to find clues. Somewhere out under the rising full moon, under the whispering cold breeze, under branches now bare of leaves ... were Missy and Muffin and Willow and four innocent puppies. And if there was a night when more dogs might be dog-napped, this was it.

They wound up and down village streets. Jack-o'-lanterns glowed on doorsteps. One lawn boasted a huge air-filled pumpkin with three smiling ghosts on top.

Chester barked nervously.

Emmaline walked up. "See? Just sniff for yourself. You don't need to be worried."

"Huh. Guess she's right," he said to Kito. "They're plastic."

They skirted the towering pine near the ice rink, its branches forming a tent above the ground.

"Hear anything?" Chester asked. "Hear Muffin this time?"

Wind whistled through the high branches and sent leaves scuttling across the road.

"Nothing more than the wind." But the memory of Muffin's ghostlike voice near this spot still made Kito jittery.

They hurried ahead and stopped at the next row of houses. As they left the last one, Chester said, "The girls must be getting tired by now."

"You'd think so."

But the girls kept going. Their canvas shoulder bags, decorated with black cats, grew bulkier with each stop, but neither girl complained of the weight. They passed the fire hydrant, dropped by Erickson's Very Fine Store for caramel apples, and continued on toward a little white house with green trim.

"C'mon," said Zoey, "the light's on."

Kito planted his feet, whined, and pulled back sharply on his leash.

Outside the house was a doghouse. Straw and big paws jutted from its dark opening.

"Spike's here! The girls don't know!" Kito barked.

But the more he pulled, the harder Zoey pulled back. "We're almost done," she said, yanking at the leash. "C'mon, Kito."

If only he could talk and warn her. If they disturbed Spike, there was no telling …

Suddenly, a low-throated rumble came from the doghouse. The butterfly and the vet turned, bumping into each other and falling down. The dogs' leashes crossed and tangled, and the more Chester tried to run, the tighter the knot they were in grew. Kito's back legs were wrapped up tight.

The growling erupted into vicious barking. Spike bulleted out of his doghouse, all teeth—and ran straight at them.

15

What Spike Knew

Despite the tangle of leashes, Kito stood ready to meet Spike's jagged jaws. He stood his ground, met Spike's mean eyes.

"Leave us alone," he said. "We aren't here to cause trouble."

The girls backed up behind his wall of defense. If ever there was chow-chow background,

"Get out of my yard!" whole body standing tal as he edged steadily clo

upward, revealing rows of sharp teeth. He snarled and snapped.

"Don't push me," Kito replied, holding steady. This wasn't the time to show a trace of fear.

"We'd run if we could," Chester hollered, "but can't you see we're in a mess here? Have pity!"

The girls were screaming and crying at the same time.

Just as Spike loomed close enough for Kito to smell his foul breath, the back door flew open.

"Spike!" shouted his owner. "Spike—come here!"

Spike glowered, his bloodshot eyes fierce with anger. He wasn't listening to his owner. He stepped forward, head down, ready to lunge.

"Now!" the woman shouted. She thumped a rolled-up newspaper in her hand. At the sound, Spike spun around. He glanced briefly over his shoulder and, tail lowered, he retreated to his doghouse.

Caroline Beyers, who ran the local hair salon, rushed to their side. "Oh, you're all a tangled mess. Here—let me help."

Soon the dogs and girls were freed. Emmaline and Zoey wiped their eyes and noses.

"Now, don't you two mind old Spike. He's really a baby when you get to know him, aren't you, Spike?"

Spike growled from his doghouse.

"Now, you girls come up to my door—oh, cute capes on your dogs, too."

Chester and Kito darted after the girls, who were standing on the top step with their Halloween bags open.

Plip-plop. Candies dropped into their bags.

"Sit," Clarice said, holding dog biscuits high. Kito and Chester obeyed and the Chewy-Chews in mi

"Thank you!"the girls called.The dogs followed them as they circled wide past Spike's doghouse and length of chain and hurried between shadows toward the sidewalk and the street. The door closed, and Clarice disappeared back inside.

"Heard Dog Watch was looking to talk to me," came Spike's voice. It sounded both menacing and friendly.

"Uh, it was discussed," Kito said.

"Schmitty came by, then chickened out," said Spike. "He ran off before he told me why he wanted to talk to me."

Keeping a safe distance on the road, Kito shifted uncomfortably. "Spike, well, have you seen anything unusual going on around this way? We're trying to locate a batch of lost puppies and three Pembrook dogs."

"Maybe. What's in it for me?"

The cool of the cement sidewalk seeped up through Kito's paws and into his bones. "re you saying you know what happened uffin and Missy and Willow and the

"Maybe."

"Could you help us with our search?"

"Maybe." A silence sliced the cool night air. Kito waited for more. The girls began pulling on their leashes.

"C'mon—let's keep going! We're not done yet!" Zoey was pulling him away down the street.

"Butcher scraps tomorrow—promise!" Kito yapped in desperation.

"You don't want to go back there!" Zoey shouted. "He'll beat you up. Now c'mon!"

"Fair enough. I heard puppies yipping— going past as I woke up from my nap. They were heading east."

Kito's collar tightened. He nearly lost his voice and had to shout. "Were they walking? In a car? What?"

Spike barked out one last reminder. "Tomorrow. Don't forget!

By then the girls had won the tug-of-war. They were heading northeast along the way making the last lonely leap in Peace toward Dr. Elizabeth's Lakeview C

her mysterious large piles of leaves.

Kito sensed trouble. They were closer than ever now to finding the missing dogs. The full moon cast pale, fingerlike shadows across the road. Wind rushed through the top boughs of pines and rattled skeletal branches. The damp air carried a hint of an early winter.

From his nose to the tip of his tail, he was filled with a horrible dread. They'd searched high and low and now Spike's news was the first solid clue. They'd find the dogs and puppies soon—he only hoped they'd find them alive.

16

Dr. Elizabeth's Home

Pembrook Beach was deserted. The breeze coming off the lake iced down Kito's back, despite his thick coat. He pulled forward, side by side with Chester, and the girls scurried behind, trying to hold fast to the leashes.

"It's so dark out!" whispered Emmaline.

"Maybe we should head back home," Zoey replied.

"But we have the dogs to protect us. We'll be okay."

109

"Yeah—and if we go around the loop we'll have made it to every house in Pembrook," Zoey said. "Our bags will be full! Let's keep going!"

Despite their candy-loaded bags, the girls ran to the only Lakeview cabin with a light on—Dr. Elizabeth's.

Kito scanned the yard, but it was free of leaf piles. She had already cleaned them up. "Nothing," he said.

"What kind of doctor was she?" Chester asked. "I thought I heard—"

"A surgeon. Retired and moved back to her hometown."

"Think she ever used dogs for medical research?" Chester whispered as the back door opened.

Dr. Elizabeth wore a bandanna over her hair and a large plastic nose with attached black glasses.

"Trick or treat!" the girls shouted.

"My—you must be the Tweet girls. Welcome to town. I heard your mother's a scientist of some sort."

"An entomologist," said Emmaline, twisting side to side so that her butterfly wings flapped.

"Oh yes, someone who studies bugs."

"Insects," Emmaline corrected her.

"Well, you girls must bring your mother and come by soon. I always serve tea at three thirty." Then she dropped candied popcorn balls into the girls' bags. "What do you say?"

"Thank you!" they chorused, then scrambled with their bags, leashes, and dogs down the steps and back to the street.

Just then, three dark shapes darted out from bushes. They were slightly smaller than adults, but bigger than kids, with frightening masks. Teenagers. "Gonna get you!" one of them cried.

"Better run home to your mommy and daddy!" another said.

They were the boys from the Spook House, all dressed in black, their faces striped. Two of them raised their arms as if they were going to take off in flight, and the third held rolls of toilet paper.

Kito growled in warning, but Zoey took off, dragging him behind her. Emmaline and Chester were way ahead.

Only pranksters, Kito realized. Their laughter faded as he rounded the loop with Zoey.

The girls only stopped running when they neared a shortcut trail through the woods. Zoey was sobbing, and Emmaline's words sounded teary. "They were after us! I've never been so scared in all my life." She kneeled down and patted Chester's head. "You led us away to safety," she said, and threw her arms around his neck.

"I have a side-ache!" Zoey whined. "I have to stop." She kneeled beside Kito and hugged him, too. "You're good dogs. You'll protect us, won't you? We love you—even if our cat doesn't."

Just then a series of muffled yips and barks sounded through the woods ahead. Wind sent leaves crackling and swirling around their feet and paws. Kito strained to ᴛ̶en, but the girls kept chattering, and he couldn't make out the dogs' voices. But he was certain he'd heard them. Distant, muffled, barely audible—and from somewhere ahead, he was sure he'd also heard Muffin's unmistakable voice. This time he was determined to find out whether it was his imagination or a ghost—or if she was alive.

Kito wriggled out of Zoey's hug and darted down the dirt path into the woods.

"What are you doing?" Chester cried out.

But Kito refused to turn back. No matter how dark the shortcut was, he was finally on the right trail.

17

Shortcut

"Wait!" Zoey cried. "Kito! Come back!"

Kito, scared though he was, padded ahead, listening, sniffing, watching for any signs of movement. Wind rustled leaves and tufts of withered grasses.

"Where is he?" came Emmaline's voice, not far behind.

"If we lose him, we're in trouble!" Chester bayed.

He and the girls were close behind. Kito quickened his pace and tried to stay ahead and stay focused. If he let himself get caught, he might be forced to turn back. This could be his last chance.

His pulse sped up. He knew Muffin and Missy, Willow and the pups were close— nearly as close as his own breath. From the trees, a pair of round and golden eyes watched him.

Kito's tail dropped down between his legs as he thudded to a stop. Whatever courage he had vanished—and he crouched low.

The eyes disappeared, and then, in a whisper of air and wings, a heavy bird swooped across his path. Kito gave a short, nervous bark, but it didn't matter. It was only an owl, and it had flown on. He'd seen them hunt before—for mice and rabbits, thankfully, not dogs.

He continued on, more slowly this time. Damp and rotting smells of leaves and moss filled his nostrils. He smelled the passing of summer, the decay of fall, the approach of deep cold. Every twitching scampering mouse and overhead squirrel drew his attention. Distractions, all. Had he imagined the voices? Were they ghosts now sent to haunt him?

In no time, the shortcut ended in pavement and he was back on the loop. The lights of an oncoming car drew near, and Kito stayed off the pavement until it passed. Just as it whizzed by, his leash tightened.

"Gotcha!" Zoey chimed. He hadn't been sharp enough. He whined, hoping she'd have sympathy and let him go.

"Don't you understand?" he whimpered, sounding as sad as he could. "I must find the puppies and Muffin and Missy and Willow. I'm sure I heard—"

"One last place," Zoey said, "and then we'll go home." She looked both ways, then ran with him across the road.

She led the way past rusty old cars, piles of freshly turned dirt, and bubbling water and minnows. They were at Howie's. No pumpkins decorated the doorstep of his mobile home. No outside lights were turned on. Only a faint light glimmered from inside.

"I can't believe he forgot about Halloween?" Chester said.

"Maybe nobody ever comes here," Kito answered. "I mean, if you were a kid, would you?"

"Probably not. It would be pretty scary."

Emmaline and Zoey didn't seem to care. They skipped up the wobbly wooden front steps and knocked.

A flurry of yipping and yapping bounced off the inside walls.

"Y'all settle down now!" one dog shouted above the others.

Kito looked at Chester, wide-eyed. "That's Muffin! Inside Howie's home!"

The girls knocked again, but still no answer came.

Kito and Chester jumped up and began clawing at the front door.

"What in the world are you

scolded. "You don't live here! Get down."

Just then, from around the shadowy corner of the mobile home, Howie lumbered toward them. Under his arm he carried something in a sack—something heavy and lifeless.

"Hi, hi, hi," he said. "My, my, my ..."

18

Lost Dogs Found

"**Kito! Chester! Fwends!**" Howie started to clap his hands and dropped his canvas sack. He picked it up again and clasped it under his big arm. "Come on! Come in!" Without an "excuse me" or "pardon me" he pushed past the girls, who nearly fell off the steps into open garbage cans.

Kito and Chester hovered on the threshold, peering in, while the girls remained on the steps with their candy sacks held open.

Kito was so surprised to see Howie, he didn't wag his tail or growl. What was he doing outside? What was going on inside? What was under his arm? Question after question raced through his head.

And there, inside, was the worst dog disaster he'd ever seen. Muffin and Missy leaped from two overstuffed chairs, their tails wagging. Willow had her paws on the kitchen counter.

"Visitors!" Muffin cried. "Why—y'all c'mon in and set awhile!"

Four puppies were rolling and chasing, yipping and yapping. They'd chewed carpets and newspapers, couch cushions and boots, to pieces. And not only had they created a chew zone a few inches deep, they had also done their puppy you-know-what in the middle of it all. Right in Howie's little living room.

"Fwends and visitors," Howie was saying to himself. He dropped the canvas bag on the kitchen table and opened the top. Out spilled nuggets of dog food, which Howie pushed onto the floor. The puppies rushed and waddled forward, their bellies round.

"My, oh my. I have more and more visitors."

Kito glanced back at Emmaline and Zoey. They were backing down the steps.

"I think he took the puppies," Zoey whispered.

"And dogs," Emmaline added.

"But they all look happy."

"Maybe."

"Chester," Kito said, as puppies covered him with kisses. "Quick. This calls for a desperate plan. If we return with the girls, how will we ever explain where the dogs and puppies are to anyone? I say we stay here—no matter what."

"What—why?" Chester wrinkled his forehead.

"Just do it."

"Okay—roger that."

The girls were on the top step, still peering inside.

"Dog food!" Zoey said. "I'm not waiting around for that!"

Emmaline pinched her nose. "Ooooh—stinks!"

They turned down the steps and called from the yard. "Kito! Chester! We have to go!"

But the two dogs didn't budge. "If we stay, they'll have to bring someone here to get us," Kito whispered. "Right?"

"I hope so."

Then the girls stopped calling and were gone.

Howie shut the door. "Cold out there."

"Joinin' our little holiday, boys?" Muffin asked.

Missy, who was much less talkative, said simply, "Glad you're here."

The door slammed behind them. They'd found the puppies. They'd found the dogs. "We're only staying for a bit," Kito said. "We've been searching high and low for you dogs—and the stolen puppies."

"Oh, sugar. Now don't get to worryin' so. No one stole nobody. Howie here just knows how to show a li'l hospitality, that's all. We've jus' been enjoyin' a li'l vacation, haven't we, Missy?"

Missy jumped back on the worn purple chair and stretched out. "But this is my chair," she said, "so don't get any ideas."

And Muffin hopped back on the plaid chair, now covered with her curly black, white, and gray fur. "Think 'bout it. When do dogs ever get a vacation from their owners, huh?"

Chester glanced at Kito. "Oh, brother! Their 'li'l vacation' has gone to their heads."

"So you mean you weren't dog-napped or stolen?" Kito asked them. "You *willingly* came here?"

In the background, Howie was squatting beside the puppies as they ate dog food from the floor. He patted their heads.

"Of course," Missy answered.

"Y'all are lookin' at us," Muffin said, rolling onto her back in the chair, "like we're plum crazy, but I'm tellin' you—we've had the time of our lives the past few days. No rules. No 'sit, stay, down' or any of that."

"And when were you planning on going home?" Chester asked.

"Oh, by and by."

"Good gravy giblets!" Chester muttered.

"And the puppies—what about them?" Kito asked. "They just disappeared from the post office steps—right into thin air."

"Oh, that Howie has a soft heart. He said they were free and he gave them a ride on his bike."

"A ride?" Chester pressed. "All four?"

"They're li'l ones, mind you. They rode in his bike baskets—probably had the most fun of their li'l lives," Muffin explained.

"Then that explains what Spike heard," said Kito. "But I heard you, Muffin, when we were searching by the ice rink...."

"Sugar, that's easy to explain. From where we're sittin', the ice rink is just on the other side of the tracks there. You probably heard some of my sweet country singin' from not so very far away."

Things were finally beginning to make some sense.

Howie looked over at Kito and Chester. "We had so much fun at Spook House! I didn't wanna leave—but you left, Kito. You pulled away fwum me!"

So that was who had hung on to his collar. Howie had held on the first time through and stayed for another round. He must have gotten over his tears about the monsters after all.

Howie tossed dog food pellets in the air. Kito sat and caught every one that sailed his way. Still, he was filled with a pang of regret. In all his quick thinking, he hadn't planned on letting the girls go the rest of the way home alone. But if his plan worked, he was counting on the girls telling Mr. and Mrs. H what had happened. And when they did, he had no doubt that his owners would come after them—and find the other dogs as well.

If his plan failed, he'd end up trapped with four mauling, kiss-happy puppies.

19

A Good Omen

As it turned out, Kito and Chester had to wait through only one program of *Animal Kingdom* at Howie's before Mr. and Mrs. H knocked on the door.

Howie opened the door. "More fwends!"

Emmaline and Zoey were right behind the Hollinghorsts.

"See?" said Zoey. "Told you we found them."

`Mr. and Mrs. H asked Howie a few questions, looked around his place, and then said, "Howie, we're going to bring more friends tomorrow and help you clean up. What do you say to that?"

"Yeah, that'd be good!" Howie said. "I like fwends!"

"Of course you do, Howie."

"And we need to get some of these dogs back to their homes. Their families are missing them."

"Sure, sure," Howie replied. "I give treats and they follow me here. I don't mind, though."

"But so many dogs—and four puppies. Fun, but lots of work, right, Howie?"

Howie nodded.

"Would you like to have one puppy all your own?" Mr. H asked.

Howie's face lit up. "My own puppy?"

"And your friends in the village can help you take care of it, like when it has to go to the vet."

Howie looked at Zoey's white jacket. "V-e-t. My puppy can see her?" Then his eyes widened. "I can read!"

Mr. and Mrs. H smiled.

• • •

Kito had never been so grateful to sleep in his own dog bed as that night. Missy and Muffin and Willow all went home to their families. After a quick call to Bud to let him know the puppies were okay, Mr. and Mrs. H drove up to Dr. Elizabeth's house with their arms full of puppies—and with a shake of her head, then a nod, Dr. Elizabeth beamed. "Oh, why not? I'll take one."

The next afternoon Kito and Chester met Howie at the end of their own driveway. "Hi! Hi! Hi!" Howie called. "We had fun—we did!"

The dogs wagged their tails in agreement.

Howie smiled and tossed the daily newspaper toward them. It spread open to the front-page photo of Howie with four puppies licking his face. The headline read:

Missing Dogs Found, Newspaper Carrier With Big Heart

"See?" Howie said, pointing to the paper. "That's me!" Then he pressed down on his bike pedal and headed toward the neighbor's house.

Kito grasped the paper in his teeth and brought it to the front door. As he did, Mr. H pulled into the driveway. He emerged from his station wagon with two puppies in his arms.

"Hey, we have a full house here," Chester said. "Cute as they are, we don't need—"

"Yeah, did you see the way they chewed that place up?"

"Don't worry, guys," Mr. H said. "Dr. Elizabeth agreed to watch these two last night, but now they've found a home. Right next door. Looks like the Tweet girls got their parents to say yes."

He sauntered across the street, the puppies licking his whiskered face the whole way.

"Well I'll be darned," Chester said.

They followed at a distance, watching as the door to the church-house opened. Emmaline and Zoey flew out and reached for the puppies in Mr. H's arms.

Emmaline held the white one. "This one's Snowball."

"Then this one's Chocolate!" said Zoey.

Mr. and Mrs. Tweet stood in the doorway, smiling. The puppies raced inside, and seconds later, with a yowling and a howling, Sheeba dashed out. She wound across the yard and zipped up the closest birch tree.

The puppies ran back outside, yipping and yapping, their tiny noses ruffling golden leaves at their feet.

"Where'd it go?" whined Snowball.

"What a fast puppy!" said Chocolate.

"I don't think that was a puppy!"

"Then what was it?"

Back arched, Sheeba glared at the puppies below her branch.

From the edge of their driveway, Kito and Chester looked on.

"Case closed on the missing dogs," said Chester, flopping to the ground, head comfortably resting on his paws. "And a cat in a tree—seems like a pretty good omen."

Kito sat back on his haunches and smiled as only dogs can do. "A good omen indeed."

Don't miss Kito and the gang's next adventure in:

Coming soon!

TOM SWIFT™

young inventor

He's smart, impossibly cool under pressure, and has more gadgets than he has time for— meet Tom Swift, Young Inventor!

From the creators of Nancy Drew and the Hardy Boys comes a series that's chock-full of adventure, high-tech gadgets, and even higher stakes. Look for a new Tom Swift adventure three times a year!

Meet Zack:

He's a genuine intergalactic space hero who fell out of the back of his own spaceship!

Join him and Omega Chimp on the silliest, zaniest, wackiest adventures this side of the Milky Way!